MOTOR MOUSE

Cynthia Rylant • Arthur Howard

Beach Lane Books

New York London Toronto Sydney New Delhi

BEACH LANE BOOKS
An imprint of Simon & Schuster Children's Publishing Division
1230 Avenue of the Americas, New York, New York 10020
Text copyright © 2019 by Cynthia Rylant
Illustrations copyright © 2019 by Arthur Howard
BEACH LANE BOOKS is a trademark of Simon & Schuster, Inc.
For information about special discounts for bulk purchases, please contact Simon & Schuster
Special Sales at 1-866-506-1949 or business@simonandschuster.com.
The Simon & Schuster Speakers Bureau can bring authors to your live event. For more
information or to book an event, contact the Simon & Schuster Speakers Bureau at
1-866-248-3049 or visit our website at www.simonspeakers.com.
Book design by Sonia Chaghatzbanian and Irene Metaxatos
The text for this book was set in Raleigh.
Manufactured in China
0219 SCP
First Edition
10 9 8 7 6 5 4 3 2 1
Library of Congress Cataloging-in-Publication Data
Names: Rylant, Cynthia, author. | Howard, Arthur, illustrator.
Title: Motor Mouse / Cynthia Rylant ; illustrated by Arthur Howard.
Description: First edition. | New York : Beach Lane Books, [2019] | Summary: Follows a busy
mouse as he drives a delivery car, enjoys Cake Day with friends, goes for a cab ride around
town, and shares popcorn with his brother at the movies.
Identifiers: LCCN 2018016839 | ISBN 9781481491266 (hardcover : alk. paper) |
ISBN 9781481491273 (e-book)
Subjects: | CYAC: Mice—Fiction.
Classification: LCC PZ7.R982 Mop 2019 | DDC [E]—dc23 LC record available at
https://lccn.loc.gov/2018016839

For dear Evie
—C. R.

For Cora Pallrand
—A. H.

CONTENTS

Motor Mouse and his friend Telly loved cake.
   "It makes me stand on my head," said Telly, standing
on his head.

Cake did not make Motor Mouse stand on his head.

But it did make him hum a little tune.

"*Hum, hum, hum,*" said Motor Mouse when he thought of cake.

Friday was Cake Day.

All week Motor Mouse and Telly did their jobs.

Motor Mouse drove his little car here and there, making deliveries.

And Telly trimmed hair (rather well).
They did their jobs, working their way to Cake Day.

But one Friday, everything went south.

Motor Mouse and Telly arrived at the Cake Shop, *and the sign said SHUT.*

"SHUT?" they shouted, waking a hedgehog on a nearby bench.

Motor Mouse and Telly were beside themselves.

"What is the point of it all without *cake*?" cried Telly.

He brought forth his handkerchief and let it all out.

Suddenly someone said, "But what about *PIE*?"
It was the hedgehog, who could not help overhearing.
"Pie?" asked Motor Mouse.
"Pie?" bubbled Telly.

The hedgehog invited them to follow behind his motorcar for some pie.

Soon they were out of town and flying over the hills.

"I AM NOT SURE I WILL LIKE PIE AS WELL AS CAKE!" shouted Telly above the roar.

Motor Mouse said nothing.
He was busy keeping up with
the hedgehog's motorcar. It
was a mighty machine.

In due time there was a village.
Then a row of shops.
Then a shop that said PIE.
"I am not sure I want to eat pie on Cake Friday," said Telly.
"We shall make do," said Motor Mouse. "Be brave."

They followed the hedgehog within.
It smelled rather good inside.
It smelled rather terribly good inside.

"Oooh," said Telly, almost feeling the
urge to stand on his head.
"*Hum,*" said Motor Mouse, "*hum, hum.*"

They looked at the case of pies.
Neither could speak.

"Allow me," said the hedgehog.
He ordered three plates of pie and three pots of tea.
They sat at a table for three.
Motor Mouse and Telly each took a bite.

"Are we dreaming?" asked Telly.
Motor Mouse checked his watch.

"No," he said.
They were indeed eating pie on Cake Friday.
And it was QUITE ACCEPTABLE.

When Motor Mouse and Telly had finished with their pie, they thanked their new friend the hedgehog for opening up a whole new world to them.

Of course, they went right back to Cake Friday the next week.

Nothing in the world but cake could ever make Telly stand on his head.

GOING FOR
A LOOK-ABOUT

Motor Mouse enjoyed his motorcar. But he could not drive and look about at everything at the same time.
He had to keep his eyes on the road.

So one day he hired a cab.

Motor Mouse said to the cabbie, "Please drive me around town. I want to have a look-about."

And he hopped in.

The cabbie had never been asked to drive someone nowhere.

Two blocks later, he stopped.

"Was that enough of a look-about?" the cabbie asked Motor Mouse.

"We hardly moved!" said Motor Mouse.

"I do not know how to drive nowhere," said the cabbie. "I need somewhere to go."

"Then what do you say we travel down Memory Lane?" said Motor Mouse.

"Let me get my map," said the cabbie.

"No, no!" said Motor Mouse. "I meant that I would like to have a look at places I remember."

"Oh, yes," said the cabbie, "I can do that very well. And what is your first place of remembering?"

Motor Mouse searched his memory.
"My dear old school," he said.

On their way to the school, Motor Mouse had a good look-about as they passed the shops and parks.

Soon they were at Motor Mouse's old school.

"Oh my," sighed Motor Mouse as he looked at the school. "The memories."

"Where next?" asked the cabbie.

"Not yet!" cried Motor Mouse. "I am having memories!"

He looked at the school and sighed again. He sighed and sighed.

"Ready anytime you are," said the cabbie.

"Memories!" cried Motor Mouse.
He sighed several times more.
Then he was done.
    "It is just that I miss my old friends,"
said Motor Mouse.

"I understand," said the cabbie. "I miss mine, too."
They both sighed.

"I say," said Motor Mouse, "perhaps Memory Lane is not the right road. Would you fancy a trip to the bowling alley instead?"

"That would be somewhere," said the cabbie.

So Motor Mouse and the cabbie drove to the bowling alley.

Motor Mouse insisted on paying for the rented shoes and bowling balls.

They each bowled quite a good game.

And when they left, neither
was thinking of old friends at all.

FRONT ROW
AT THE
PICTURE SHOW

otor Mouse and his brother, Valentino, loved the picture show. They were always there on Saturdays for the first matinee.

The brothers usually agreed on what show to see. And they were in perfect agreement about the best place to sit (front row, hands down).

But they could never see eye to eye on the snacks.
Specifically, the popcorn.
The biggest bucket was the best deal at the picture show.
Valentino loved a deal, so he always wanted to buy a big bucket to share with Motor Mouse, instead of a small bucket for each of them.

This had not worked for years. And it was not working
this Saturday, either.

"The biggest bucket has not worked for years!" said
Motor Mouse. "And that is because you hog it!"

"I do not," said Valentino.

"We could each have our own small bucket," said Motor Mouse. "And here we are once again, with this thing between us."

"I promise to share," said Valentino.

"You will not share," said Motor Mouse. "You forget to share. You watch the show and hog the bucket."

"I don't," said Valentino, his arms tightly wrapped around the bucket.

"You do," said Motor Mouse. "So this time, unpeel yourself from the bucket."

Valentino frowned and let his brother take the bucket. When they sat down in the front row, Valentino looked at his empty lap.

"I feel so empty," he said.

"Nonsense," said Motor Mouse. "Here, dig in."
Valentino reached across the armrest.
He put a few feeble morsels of popcorn into his mouth.
"Popcorn is a bit like air when you're not the one holding the bucket," said Valentino.

"Nonsense," said Motor Mouse. "We will share. We will cooperate. We will co-own the bucket."

Valentino shook his head. "Empty," he said.

Motor Mouse looked at his brother's sad face.

"Oh for Pete's sake," said Motor Mouse. He stood up and put the biggest bucket into Valentino's lap.

"Really?" Valentino said, brightening right up.

"I will be back," said Motor Mouse.

Soon he was back, and he had another biggest bucket.
"This one is for me," Motor Mouse told Valentino.

"Why not the small bucket for you?" asked Valentino.

"You are right," said Motor Mouse. "The biggest bucket is the best deal."

Valentino beamed.

Motor Mouse and Valentino watched the picture show with not even one tiny moment of hogging.

And when the show was over, between them there was not even one tiny kernel of popcorn left.

"Amazing," said Motor Mouse. "I did not know I could eat so much popcorn."

"Oh, it's not hard," said Valentino. "I have done it many . . ."

Valentino stopped. He looked at Motor Mouse.

"Oops," said Valentino. "I guess I do hog."

"But you always buy us ice cream after the show," said Motor Mouse. "And I always order two scoops."

"And I always order just one!" said Valentino.

"And you also treat my friends when we see them," added Motor Mouse.

"I do!" said Valentino.

"You are a fine brother," said Motor Mouse.

"Thank you," said Valentino.

He could not now even recall the feeling of empty.

Motor Mouse and Valentino got into the motorcar and headed for the ice cream shop.

Life was full.